Make a Diorama for a Tiger

Jonathon Phillips
Photographs by Lindsay Edwards

Contents

Dioramas

Dioramas are **scenes** created in a box.
They are used to entertain and **inform** people about a topic.

This large diorama is in a museum and shows wildlife in their natural environment.

You can make your own diorama using some simple materials found at home, such as a shoebox, magazines and coloured markers.

To begin, you will need a topic. This could be anything, for example, space, dinosaurs or events from history.

The following procedure shows how to make a diorama of a Sumatran tiger's **habitat**. Sumatran tigers are found on the island of Sumatra, in Indonesia. They live in thick, grassy forests on mountains and in **lowlands**, where tall trees block out most of the sunlight. Here, the tigers can **stalk** their prey and hide from humans.

Goal

To make a diorama of a Sumatran tiger's forest habitat

Materials

You will need:

- library books or access to the internet (for researching your topic)

- a large cardboard shoebox (lid removed)

- an A3 piece of white paper
- a sharp pencil

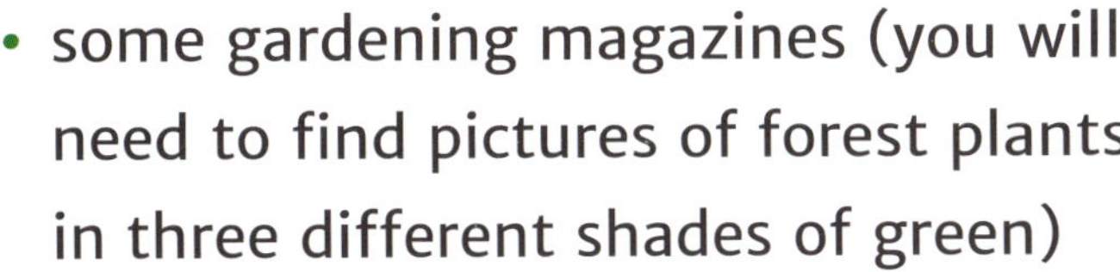

- some gardening magazines (you will need to find pictures of forest plants in three different shades of green)

- scissors

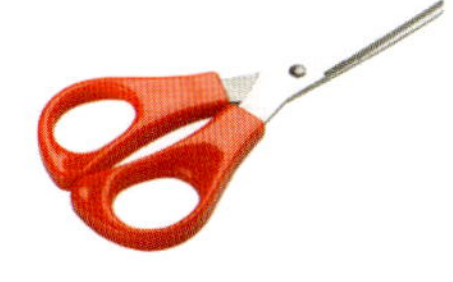

- glue

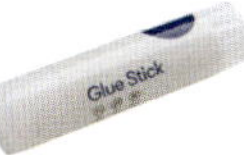

- green and brown wool

- tape

- an A5 piece of stiff white card (about 15 cm × 21 cm)

- coloured markers

- a lamp
- an A4 piece of white paper and a pen.

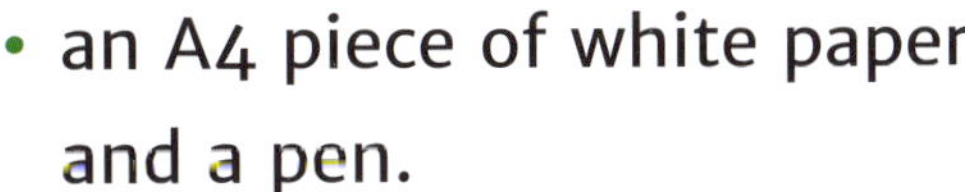

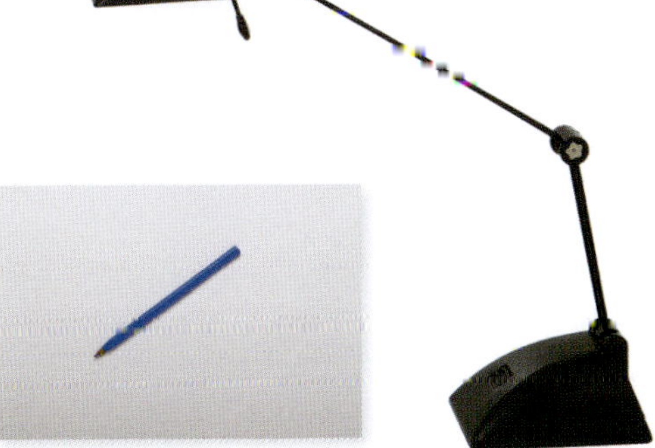

Steps

Researching Your Topic

1. Begin by researching your topic. Search in library books or on the internet to find photos of Sumatran tigers in their forest habitat.

2. Look closely at the colours and **textures** in the pictures you find.

Notice how it is dark inside a Sumatran forest. Small spots of light shine through the gaps in the treetops. This is called "dappled" light.

Planning Your Diorama

1. Turn your shoebox on its side, so that the opening is facing towards you. Think about how you will use the space inside the box to make your forest habitat.
2. On your A3 piece of paper, use your pencil to draw a rectangle that is about the same size as your shoebox.

3. Divide the rectangle into three even spaces. The space at the front will be the **foreground** of your diorama. The space in the middle will be the **middle ground**. The space at the back will be the background.

4. Draw roughly where you plan to put the grass and tigers in your diorama. The things you place in the background will need to look like they are far away. Make them smaller and less brightly coloured than the things in the middle ground or foreground.

Use your drawing as a guide for the rest of the project.

Making the Forest Habitat

1. Look through the gardening magazines for photos of green plants. These are for the background of your diorama, so try to find light-coloured plants. Remember: things that are further away appear lighter and more **faded** than those closer up.
2. Cut the pictures out and glue them to the inside back, sides and bottom of the shoebox.

3. Next, make some grass to put into the middle ground of your diorama. Find some pictures of green plants that are a bit darker than your background plants.

4. Cut the pictures into shapes so they look like grass.

5. Take a grass shape and fold it along the bottom, then unfold it halfway. This will create a thin, flat strip called a "tab".

6. Put some glue onto the tab and stick it in the middle ground of your diorama, so it is standing up. Do the same with your other grass shapes.

7. Next, make some grass to put in the foreground. Find some pictures of forest plants in the darkest green colour. Cut them into grass shapes.

8. Once again, fold along the bottom of the grass to create a tab. Glue the tabs of grass into the foreground of your diorama, standing upright.

9. Make some **vines** for your forest habitat.
Cut some pieces of green and brown wool
about 20 to 30 centimetres long.
Tape the pieces of wool to the ceiling of the shoebox
and let them dangle down to look like vines.

10. Next, take the sharp pencil and poke holes in the top of the shoebox. This will allow spots of light to fall through into the diorama.

Making the Sumatran Tigers

1. Take the piece of stiff card and cut it into two rectangles. Make one rectangle smaller than the other.
2. Fold each rectangle in half, lengthways.

3. On one side of the larger piece of card, use your pencil to draw a side-on picture of a Sumatran tiger. (You can copy a picture you found in a book or on the internet when you were doing your research.) Make sure the top of the tiger's back runs along the fold in the card.

4. Colour in the tiger using coloured markers. To show the colour of the tiger's coat, try drawing some yellow, orange and brown stripes, side by side.

5. Keeping the card folded, cut around the outside of the tiger. Make sure that you cut through the two layers of card, but leave the top of the tiger's back uncut.

6. Fold out the card so the tiger stands up.

7. Repeat steps 3 to 6 with the smaller piece of card.

Putting Your Diorama Together

1. Place the smaller tiger in the middle ground of your diorama, behind some grass, but not completely hidden.

2. Then, place the larger tiger in the foreground of your diorama, near some grass.

3. Place a lamp above your diorama. Turn the lamp on. The holes in the top of the shoebox will make the light in your diorama seem dappled.

4. Last, write some information about the Sumatran tiger and its habitat on the folded A4 piece of paper. Use the glue to attach it to the side of your diorama, to explain what your diorama shows.

You now have a diorama that shows the viewer what the habitat of the Sumatran tiger looks like!

Glossary

faded (*adjective*)	having lost some of its colour
foreground (*noun*)	the area at the front of a place or setting
habitat (*noun*)	the place where animals usually live
inform (*verb*)	to give information about a topic
lowlands (*noun*)	land that is lower than the land around it
middle ground (*noun*)	the area in the middle of a place or setting
scenes (*noun*)	images of a place or area
stalk (*verb*)	to follow prey slowly and quietly
textures (*noun*)	the ways things feel and look; either rough or smooth
vines (*noun*)	thin-stemmed plants that grow by climbing on and around things